DORA the EXPLORER

The Birthday Dance

Daisy's Fiesta de Quinceañera

adapted by Alison Inches
based on the original teleplay "Daisy, La Quinceañera"
by Valerie Walsh
illustrated by Dave Aikins

Simon Spotlight/Nick Jr.
New York   London   Toronto   Sydney

Based on the TV series *Dora the Explorer*® as seen on Nick Jr.®

SIMON SPOTLIGHT
An imprint of Simon & Schuster Children's Publishing Division
1230 Avenue of the Americas, New York, New York 10020
© 2006 Viacom International Inc. All rights reserved.
NICK JR., *Dora the Explorer*, and all related titles, logos, and characters are
registered trademarks of Viacom International Inc.
All rights reserved, including the right of reproduction in whole or in part in any form.
SIMON SPOTLIGHT and colophon are registered trademarks of Simon & Schuster, Inc.
Manufactured in the United States of America
First Edition
2 4 6 8 10 9 7 5 3 1
ISBN-13: 978-1-4169-1303-0
ISBN-10: 1-4169-1303-3

¡Hola! I'm Dora, and this is Boots. Today we're going to my cousin Daisy's fifteenth birthday party—her *fiesta de quinceañera.* That's a special birthday party where she'll become all grown up!

Boots and I need your help to deliver Daisy's present—her special crown and shoes—to wear at her party. She can't start the party without them!

Will you help us take the crown and shoes to Daisy's *fiesta de quinceañera?*
Great!

Map says we have to go past the Barn and then through the Rainforest to get to Daisy's party!

Remember to watch out for that sneaky fox, Swiper. He may try to swipe Daisy's present. If you see him, say "Swiper, no swiping!" *¡Vámonos!* Let's go!

There's the Barn! Hey—do you see that funny-looking duck?

Wait—that's not a duck! It's Swiper the fox!

Oh, no! Swiper swiped Daisy's present and threw it on that conveyor belt. It's rolling away! We have to get Daisy's present back.

If the present is on the conveyor belt with a circle flap, say "*¡Círculo!*" If the present is on the conveyor belt with a triangle flap, say "*¡Triángulo!*"

Quick! Which conveyor belt is the present on?

¡Círculo! ¡Sí!

We got Daisy's present back *and* we made it past the Barn.
Thanks for helping! Now we need to go through the Rainforest.
But look! There's a rain cloud over the Rainforest. We can't let
Daisy's present get wet!

Do you see something in my Backpack that can keep us dry in the Rainforest?

¡Sí! ¡El paraguas! The umbrella! That can keep us dry. Good thinking!

We made it through the Rainforest without getting wet! And there's my cousin Diego with Baby Jaguar. Diego is Daisy's brother.

¡Hola, primo!

Diego is on his way to Daisy's *fiesta de quinceañera* too.

We can go together!

Come on!

Ding! Dong! Ding! Dong!
The bells are ringing! It's time for Daisy's party. But the party can't start without us because we have Daisy's crown and shoes!

We need to hurry! Diego says the giant condor birds can fly us to the party quickly.

Look—there's the party! And there's my cousin Daisy. Happy birthday, Daisy! We have your special crown and shoes, so you can start *la fiesta de quinceañera*!

But first Boots and I need to put on our fancy party clothes too!

Now it's time for the ceremony to begin. Daisy's *mami* is crowning her with the special crown we brought to her. Daisy's *papi* is helping her into her grown-up shoes. Wow, Daisy really *does* look all grown up!

Now it's time for Daisy and her *papi* to walk arm in arm down the aisle. Let's clap and cheer for Daisy!

Now it's time for dancing! Let's all do the mambo dance.
I love to mambo! Do you want to mambo with us?

Here's how you do it:
First march in place . . .
then wiggle your hips . . .
now wave your hands in the air!
You're doing the mambo!

Mambo! Mambo! We did it! Thanks for helping us get to Daisy's party. We couldn't have done it without you!